The Devil's Quest

A Christmas Vessel

Kaitlyn McKnight

For everyone who has ever been deceived.

Foreword

Once again, this young adult writer pulls us into a world of mystery and magic. At first you think you know the story and its origin, but, to an unpredictable delight, it is a welcomed twist on an old favorite. The vivid imagination of this poem allows us to look outside of the norm and be maladaptive without guilt. There is a uniqueness to capture your attention and fuel the need to keep reading. This poem of a story gives you a brief look into malevolence that is shrouded from virtue, and hidden goodness is revealed as a foe is brought to light. The idiosyncratic mind of Kaitlyn McKnight has bestowed upon us this unusual poem that lets us travel into a world of obscurity and surprise.

HAPPY READING

The Devil's Quest
A Christmas Vessel

And so, Satan looked high above his place and listened.

To the sound of merriment and holiday praise

"I curse this time of the year" the devil exclaimed.

"With its worship and cheer, it sets me aflame."

Then he arose from his low place

And soared to heaven and stood before the pearly gates.

"Lo, lo" he began "hear me you there, angel.

"Go and tell your God I have come to seek counsel."

"Away now, Satan" the angel responded.

"Heaven has no time now for your incessant annoyance."

"I say again to you, oh faithful servant to your Master.

"Go and tell your God I have come for quite a mat-ter."

So, the angel did as the devil requested.

And that sly trickster was brought before God with his message.

"Oh God of Abraham, Isaac, and Jacob" the trickster began with a smirk.

"Have pity on me, I cannot stand my hurt."

"What say ye, Satan?" Our Almighty God questioned.

And the devil said "This time of the year, I can't bear the whole season.

"So have me let it end, let me go and seek and devour.

"The one You use for this seasonal hour.

"That one man You have, the goodwill bearer.

"Kris Kringle, Saint Nick, that Santa Claus character

"You have turned him previous into Your servant.

"Spreading his holiday sermon of Your Son

"And family and joy and giving galore.

"Oh, Master of heaven let me visit him at his door.

"I will with one trick take Christmas from him.

"Then spread my sin across the realm."

And God listened and then said "My people are faithful, strong and have might.

"They fly on eagles and soar higher than the mounts."

"So, I will allow you to go forth with your trick.

"Try to take Christmas from My servant, Saint Nick

"And try to spread your sin through the villages."

And the devil "Woohooed!" and leaped down to earth.

He took the form of a man with a mingled beard and a mouth most crooked.

And his coat was deep crimson, and his eyes were green.

And in the distance, he saw the lights' gleam.

And he approached further and saw a building most merry.

With a workshop and stables and a house with a grand chimney

All were white as covered by God's raiment.

So, from a distance Satan in disguise

Took in a deep breath and yelled with all his might.

"Lo, lo come forth I bear a message, a surprise!"

And the door to the workshop opened in seconds.

To reveal an elf in his own white outfit

And the elf peered and squinted his eyes.

Then asked in his calm voice "Who is it? Who's there? What surprise?"

And Satan said "'Tis I one sent from God.

"I've come to see Kris Kringle, where is Santa Claus?"

"He is resting" said the elf still looking in the distance.

"Come closer, man of God, I cannot see your eyes, come closer I insist it."

"My eyes, that's rather strange" Satan said still sitting in the snow.

"That may be, but the devil is about, we sensed him in the air not long ago."

Then the elf continued "He must have come to disrupt the holiday flow"

"Or destroy the whole thing" that old trickster added.

"Which is why your eyes are so important.

"For Satan changes form from man to bear.

"But he cannot fool with his eyes those who stare.

"Whether brown, blue, or even green

"The devil cannot hide his true being."

"Is that so" the devil said knee deep now in the snow and dread.

"Now go get the resting man from bed.

"And tell him God has sent me in his stead.

"Come to the house" the elf offered.

"Come and get warmed by the fire and with some hot chocolate."

And the devil approached the house God had cloaked.

And kept his head low as he entered the abode.

Then all of a sudden, the silence was broken.

With the sound of Christmas hymns most joyous

Satan was hearing the workshop elves sing.

And his hands went to his ears, and he stifled a scream.

"Curse it all, this whole Christmas thing!

"Ah, but in a moment, I will be rid of the whole thing.

"I will get Saint Nick with a dirty trick.

"And that good tidings man won't get out of it!"

Then a door opened and out walked a man
With a belly like a drum and a beard that hung down to his hands
And the devil faced the mantle with his back to the man.
And then Satan said "Lo, lo Santa Claus, I come with a plan."
And the rosy cheeked man stroked his beard for a moment.
"Is that so, man of God, what is intended?"

Satan snickled to himself before saying "This holiday season, this Christmas time.
"It's tiring, yes with the joy giving and flying.
"Well, I have been sent to take your place for the night.

"Is this so" Santa Claus wondered.

"Oh, why yes of course and I won't fumble."

Then the devil said more "You see this red coat and beard?

"I'm ready for the reindeer, the gift giving, the cheer."

Then Santa said "Well if God commanded these things"

And without another word Satan made haste to the workshop with glee

He entered at once not showing his face "Lo, lo" he hissed.

Interrupting the work and the praise

"Prepare the gifts, prepare the sleigh."

And in no time at all Satan, still in disguise

Was helped in the sleigh and laughed a few times.

Then he grabbed the reigns and did a loud sigh

Then feeling victorious in that very moment

He turned his head to the elves and Santa.

And they all saw his eyes that were truly dark and spiraling.

And the devil said "Lo, lo, Merry Christmas indeed."

And Satan snapped the reigns, and the reindeer flew away.

There was such a long pause.

Santa and the elves just stood there.

Then Santa broke the silence

"I was tricked.

"The devil came, and he played a trick.

"He was right before me, and I didn't know.

"Now he's off to destroy the Son's birthday.

"The day of family, of gathering, of remembering our Savior."

And while those at the North Pole stood feeling defeated

Satan was high above

"Now let's see, what's first?"

He looked through the sack.

"Sheet music I see.

"These are hymns about God.

"Oh, no, no, no I can't have this."

And he changed the notes to resemble some chant that pleased his ears.

Then he dropped the music and watched it float down a chimney

"Now here is a Bible all nice and new."

And he began ripping pages out of the Book.

Then he sent it tumbling down another chimney

"And this pure trumpet" he sneered.

And blew in it once turning its once merry tune to one that became foul.

And down the trumpet went into another chimney.

Then daybreak occurred and all began to awake

And rush down to their new presents

And Satan flew back to Santa Claus and the elves.

The trickster jumped out of the sleigh with an empty sack.

Then smiled and said "Lo, lo, Merry Christmas, indeed!" at the top of his voice.

He threw the sack to the ground "I tricked you without hassle!

"I stood before you all who said you sensed me coming.

"And yet I still deceived you! I have won!

"I have ruined your little Christmas.

"With the gifts I have changed, the people will be in confusion.

"And but then, lo, lo they will play with my gifts.

"They will test them just to see.

"And then they won't be able to stop them-selves!

"They'll play with the sin; they'll enjoy the feeling I've given.

"And in no time, they'll forget God and the true meaning of Christmas altogether."

After the gloating Santa Claus said "Satan, I rebuke you."

With burning ears, the devil responded, "Speak truly, you've lost to me."

But Santa shook his head "No, that is where you are wrong.

"There is victory in Jesus.

"When you flew off yes, we all felt beaten.

"But now I've only just remembered God's Word

"Where it says, 'pray without ceasing.'"

Then Santa Claus turned to the elves whose expressions were still blue

"That is what we must do.

"Let us kneel and hold hands and ask God to let His light shine through."

So, they knelt and held hands ignoring Satan's blasphemy.

And Kris Kringle said, "Now repeat after me."

Almighty God, we come to you now. First, we thank you for giving your Son that we may have salvation. Now, oh God, we ask for the strength to overcome all of Satan's tricks. The devil is cunning, and we are weak, but with You, Lord, the devil's deceit can be defeated. Satan has come and laid out his traps that we might be snared in his sin and forget You, but God, please let this entrapment not come to pass. Help us to put down that which sinfully beckons us and keep us your servants' minds on each of our purposes and service. Amen.

Then all of a sudden, Satan hollered.

"Why do I feel such pain, why am I bothered!?

"It was the prayer that was prayed, the sincerity in it!"

And so, all around the world the people felt it.

The Spirit of God covered the earth like a blanket.

And the people put down the sins the devil had sent them.

This story, its message is one that is rather simple.

Don't let Satan make you forget what Christmas is.

Santa Claus here acted as God's vessel.

As we all are to spread His message

Satan will come to you in disguise.

But use God's Spirit in you to see the devil's eyes.

Because a 'gift' from Satan is not one pleasant

So never, ever, ever think to open it.

But when the sin does happen to take you

Pray without ceasing that God will save you!

And now this story will end like this.

Kaitlyn McKnight

Merry Christmas to all and forget not Jesus Christ.

About the Author

Kaitlyn McKnight started her writing journey at the age of twelve as a class assignment. Her writing assignment grew into the Zodiac Saga trilogy. That was her breakout into the world of storytelling. She was born to military parents and raised in Mississippi. She enjoys creating a multiplicity of characters with unique traits. Her funny, sometimes serious, and quirky personality make her relatable to everyone who meets her. Kaitlyn's stories are filled with charm, devotion, unpredictability, and some maleficence. Her writings are enjoyed by tweens, teens, and adults of all ages.

www.ingramcontent.com/pod-product-compliance
Lightning Source LLC
Chambersburg PA
CBHW042035120726
47911CB00027B/748